This book belongs to

....

For Rohan, Sajjan and Veer – R.S.

For my amazing mum, Hazell – L.D.

HODDER CHILDREN'S BOOKS
First published in Great Britain in 2022
by Hodder and Stoughton

10 9 8 7 6 5 4 3 2

Text © Ranj Singh, 2022
Illustrations © Hachette Children's Group, 2022
Illustrated by Liam Darcy

A CIP catalogue record for this book is available from the British Library.

ISBN 978 1 44496 506 3

Printed and bound in China

MIX
Paper from
responsible sources
FSC® C104740
FSC www.fsc.org

HODDER CHILDREN'S BOOKS
An imprint of Hachette Children's Group
Part of Hodder and Stoughton
Carmelite House, 50 Victoria Embankment,
London EC4Y 0DZ

An Hachette UK Company
www.hachette.co.uk
www.hachettechildrens.co.uk

A SUPERPOWER
Like Mine

Dr Ranj

Illustrated by Liam Darcy

Hodder
Children's
Books

Femi and her daddy **loved** playing **superheroes** together.

Daddy would help Femi to **FLY** using his super-strength!

Sometimes, she turned **INVISIBLE,** and Daddy couldn't see her!

Femi loved it most when Daddy let her turn him into **STICKERMAN!**

"I wish I had *real* superpowers," said Femi one afternoon.

"But you do!" said Dad. "Superpowers can't always be seen. Sometimes they're the things **INSIDE** you that make you special."

Femi had never thought about having superpowers on the inside.

"The people around us can bring out those things," added Dad.
"Think about what makes others special to you, and maybe
you'll find some clues about your own real superpowers too."

So Femi started thinking . . .

"My big sister Fara is the **FUNNIEST** person I know, and she has taught me lots of jokes too."

"Granny always says you should take to the stage as a double act!" said Dad.

"I think we have the power to **MAKE THE WHOLE WORLD LAUGH!**" added Femi.

"What about your friend Rohan?" said Dad. "What qualities does he inspire in you?"

"Rohan is so smart – he remembers **EVERYTHING!** He doesn't say much but, when we play together, we can solve puzzles in **SECONDS**," said Femi. "We could be the world's best codebreakers. Maybe my power is my **BRAIN!**"

RABBIT FOOD

"Then there's my friend Oscar," said Femi. "He's **KIND** and **CARING.** He likes to talk to animals and always makes sure the class bunnies are looked after."

"You love caring for them together," said Dad.

"We do!" said Femi. "He's shown me the power of **KINDNESS!**"

"And what about Finn?" asked Dad.
"You didn't want to leave when I came
to collect you from your playdate!"

"Finn is creative and makes up the
BEST games. Once, he even flew us
to the moon!" said Femi. "His mummies
say we are lucky to have the
POWER OF IMAGINATION."

"You're great at this," laughed Dad. "Who else?"

"My teacher, Miss Cheung!" said Femi. "She is always patient. She never gets cross or frustrated, even when we all have the wiggles and can't sit still! She showed me the **POWER OF PATIENCE . . .**

. . . because sometimes you have to wait to wiggle!"

"Oh, and Amba! She's the **BRAVEST** person I know. She's not scared of **ANYTHING.**

We climb mountains,

hunt ghosts . . .

. . . and travel through **jungles.**

We're going to be explorers," said Femi.
"You have to be **BRAVE** to **DREAM BIG!**"

"You're certainly full of courage," said Dad.

"And you're a good **LISTENER,** Daddy," said Femi.
"You always let me share what I'm thinking about.

People have told me I'm a good listener too.
I think that's because of you, **SUPERDAD!**"

"I have **SUPERFRIENDS,**

a **SUPERSISTER**

and I definitely have a
SUPERPET!

There are **SUPERDOCTORS,**

SUPERTEACHERS

and **SUPERCARERS.**

SUPERDANCERS

and **SUPERPAINTERS!**

SUPERLIBRARIANS

and **SUPERSHOPKEEPERS!**

I have a **SUPERGRANNY**

and two
SUPERGRANDADS!"

"Exactly!" said Dad. "And they all help to shape you and bring out your best powers – **KINDNESS, IMAGINATION, BRAVERY, CLEVERNESS, SMILES AND SO MUCH MORE!**"

"Thanks, Daddy! I **DO** have superpowers. But I know what my very **BEST** superpower is," said Femi. "It's . . .

. . . BEING ME!

Super Femi!"

I am so proud of this book in so many ways. It wouldn't have
happened without the superpowers of some lovely people who
have made it what it is. So a huge thank you to Liam Darcy,
Elaine Connolly, Katie Sassienie and Izzy Jones. Also a big thank
you to James McParland, Sarah Rhodes, KT Forster and Craig
Latto. And of course, all the amazing superheroes who have
inspired it. You all make the world a little bit more wonderful.

Dr Ranj